WHITE
IS
THE MOON

For Anthony and Sarah

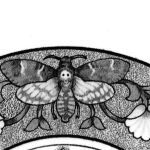

WHITE
IS
THE MOON

Valerie Greeley

Macmillan Publishing Company   New York

Maxwell Macmillan International Publishing Group
New York   Oxford   Singapore   Sydney

White is the moon
Shining bright
Sees an owl
In the night

Brown is the owl
With steely stare
Sees a fox
Standing there

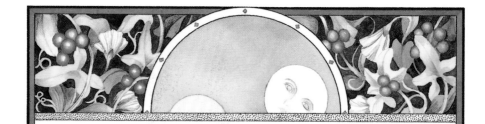

Red is the fox
Sly and fast
Sees a frog
Hopping past

Green is the frog
With glinting eyes
Sees the sun
Slowly rise

Yellow's the sun
Golden, bright
Sees a bird
Taking flight

Black is the bird
Swooping low
Sees a crab
Down below

Pink is the crab
Crawling up
Sees a seal
With her pup

Gray is the seal
Shining wet
Sees the sun
About to set

Orange the sun
Changing hue
Sees the sky
Changing too

Blue is the sky
In fading light
Sees the moon
Now say Goodnight!

Macmillan Publishing Company
866 Third Avenue, New York, NY 10022

Collier Macmillan Canada, Inc.
1200 Eglinton Avenue East, Suite 200, Don Mills, Ontario M3C 3N1

First published in 1990 by Blackie and Son Limited, London, England
First American Edition 1991   Printed in Hong Kong

10 9 8 7 6 5 4 3 2 1

Library of Congress CIP data is available
ISBN 0-02-736915-3

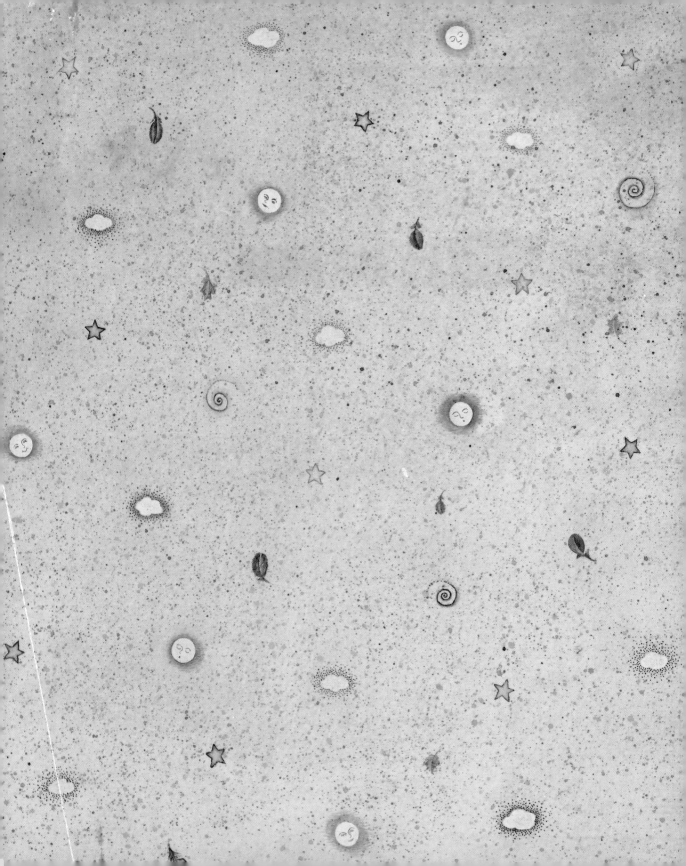